SMILE

To my Challenge girls, with love and gratitude. — TM

To my amazing mother, Debbie — who continues
to make me smile, even after a good cry. — JR

SOMETIMES —
A LOT OF SOMETIMES —
I WANT TO SMILE.

IT COULD BE ...

A COSY UNDER BLANKET SMILE.

A SWEETIE-PIE WINK SMILE.

Home
Sweet
Home

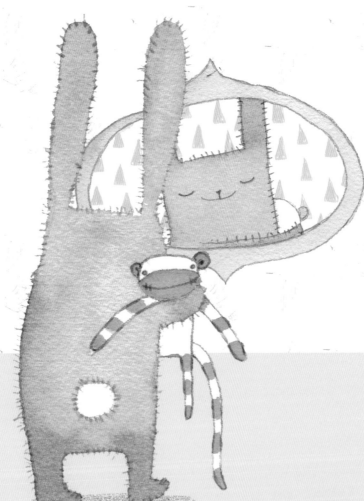

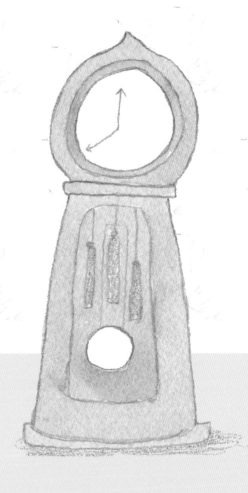

A **HUG** A **CUDDLY MONKEY** SMILE.

A **WHAT TO DO NOW?** SMILE.

AN ATE ALL THE PIES SMILE.

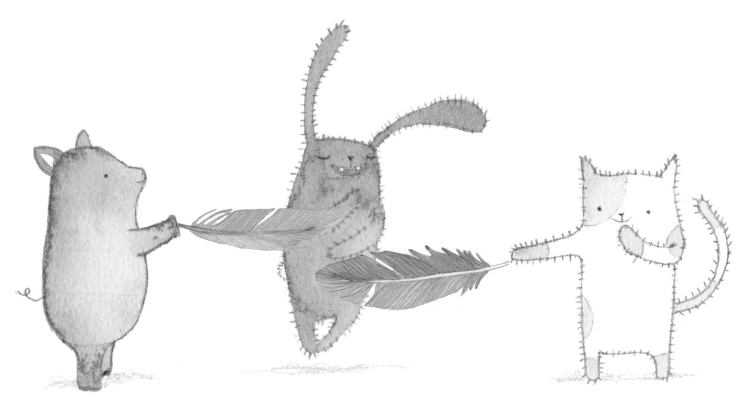

A **SILLY** SMILE.

A WALKING IN THE FOREST SMILE.

A LAUGH TILL YOU CRY SMILE.

A **THIS WILL BE GOOD** SMILE.

PERHAPS IT'S A SPINNING ROUND-AND-ROUND SMILE.

A QUIET WITH THE NIGHTLIGHT SMILE.

OR MAYBE, JUST MAYBE, IT'S . . .

A WRAPPED IN A CUDDLE SMILE.

OR MAYBE, JUST MAYBE, IT'S . . .

A WRAPPED IN A CUDDLE CRY.

AN I DIDN'T MEAN IT CRY.

"LOOK OUT!" CRY A

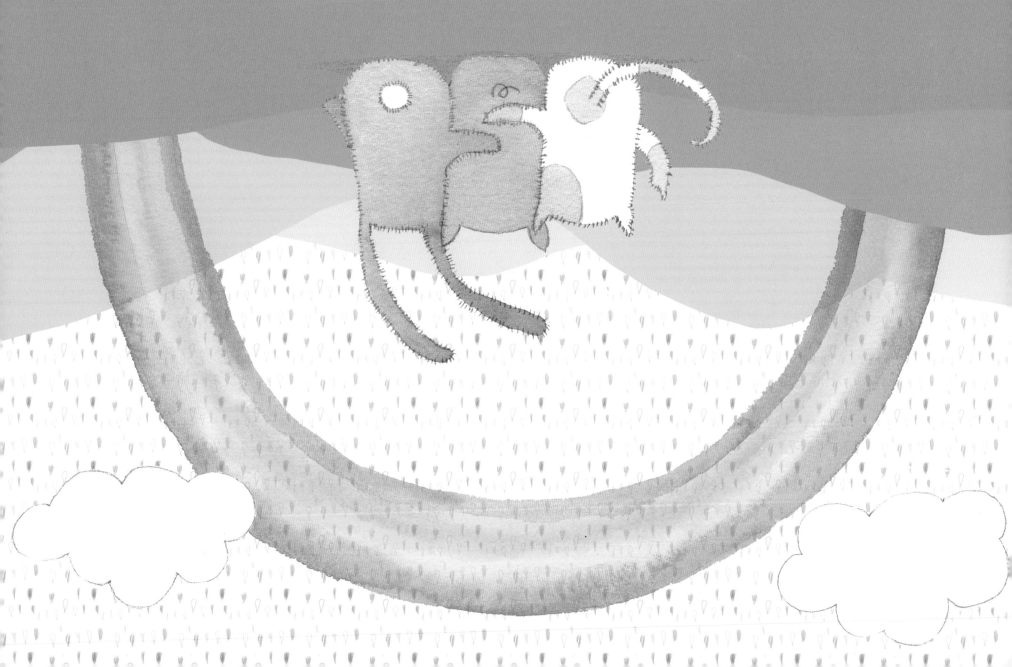

AN OH MY, THIS IS LOVELY CRY,

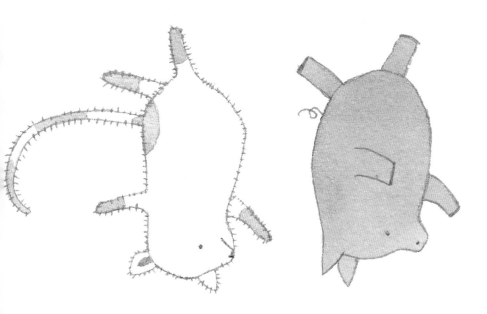

A GOODBYE CRY.

A BALLOON **POP** CRY.

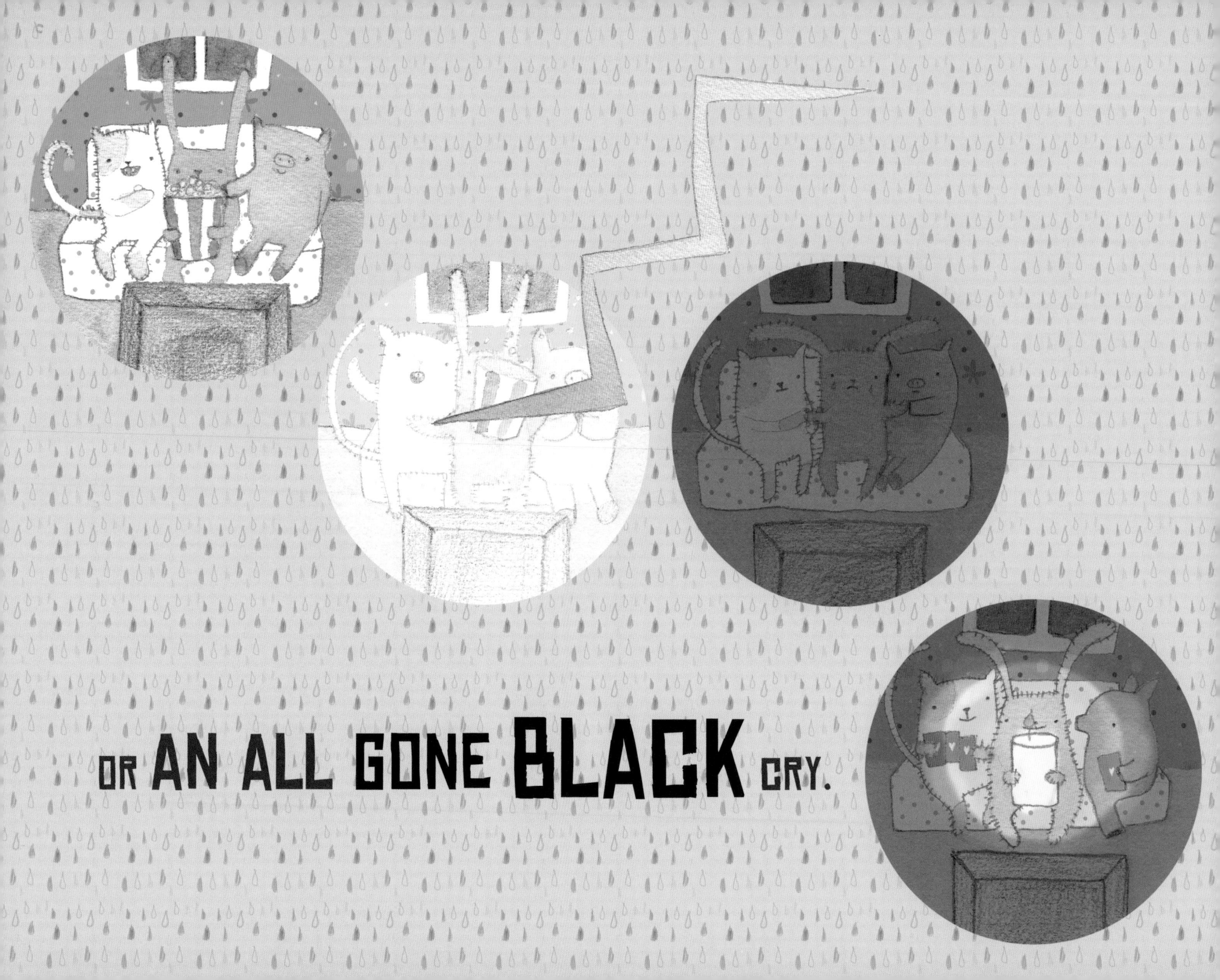

OR **AN ALL** GONE **BLACK** CRY.

A TICKLE CRY.

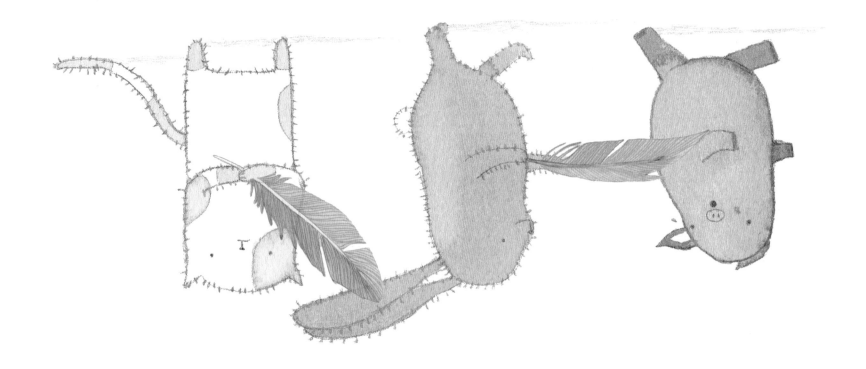

PERHAPS IT'S A LOST CRY.

A **TUTU IN THE WASH** CRY.

A NEED A BANDAGE QUICK CRY.

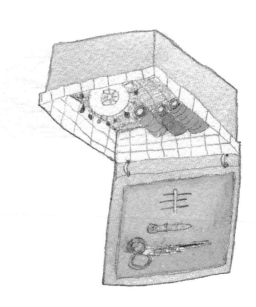

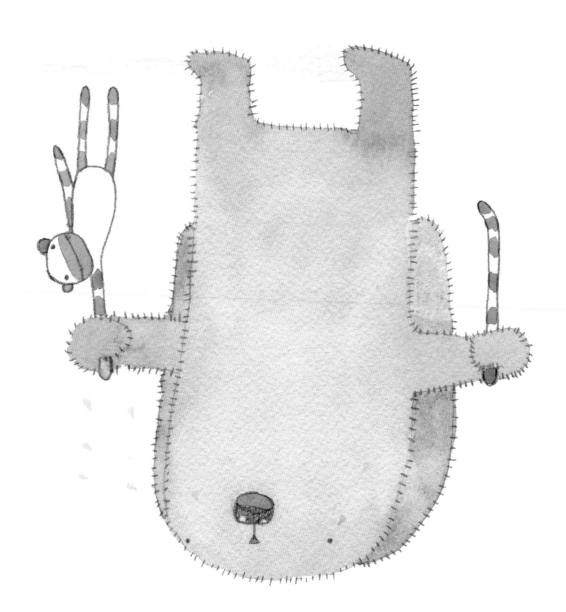

AN ICE-CREAM PLOPPING  DOWN CRY.

SOMETIMES — JUST SOMETIMES — I WANT TO **CRY**.

IT MIGHT BE ...

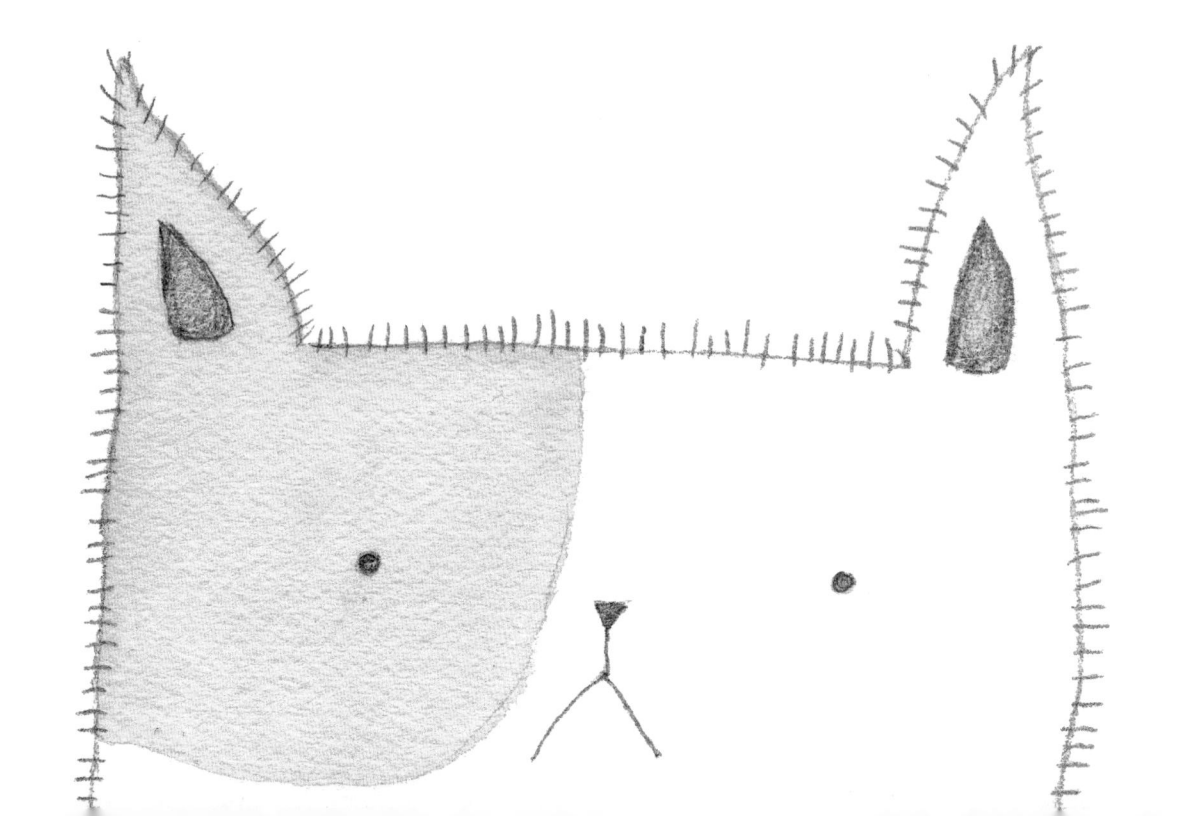

First published 2016

EK Books
an imprint of Exisle Publishing Pty Ltd
'Moonrising', Narone Creek Road, Wollombi, NSW 2325, Australia
P.O. Box 60–490, Titirangi, Auckland 0642, New Zealand
www.ekbooks.com.au

A CiP record for this book is available from the National Library of Australia.

ISBN 978-1-921966-98-9

Designed by Big Cat Design
Typeset in Chinese Rocks 27 on 35pt leading
Printed in China
This book uses paper sourced under ISO 14001 guidelines from
well-managed forests and other controlled sources.

2 4 6 8 10 9 7 5 3 1

GRY